READER COLLECTION

LEGO

NINJAGO
Masters of Spinjitzu

BASED ON THE HIT TV SERIES!

SECRETS OF SPINJITZU

BY TRACEY WEST & KATE HOWARD

LEGO® Ninjago: Pirates vs. Ninja (978-0-545-60800-8) © 2013 The LEGO Group.
LEGO® Ninjago: The Green Ninja (978-0-545-60798-8) © 2013 The LEGO Group.
LEGO® Ninjago: Attack of the Nindroids (978-0-545-64390-0) © 2014 The LEGO Group.
LEGO® Ninjago: Techno Strike! (978-0-545-66384-7) © 2014 The LEGO Group.

ISBN 978-1-4351-5840-5

12 11 10 9 8 7 6 5 4 3 2 1   14 15 16 17 18 19/0
Printed in Singapore   46
This edition first printing, October 2014

SCHOLASTIC INC.

PATIENCE, LLOYD!

"*Hii-yah!* Fists of Fury!" Lloyd yelled, pounding his fist into Kai's palm.

Ninja Cole, Jay, Kai, and Zane were training Lloyd in their Ninjago™ City apartment. It had been their home since evil Lord Garmadon had stolen the *Destiny's Bounty*, their flying ship. But a kitchen was no place to train a ninja. Kai had to use oven mitts for gloves.

"Lloyd, you are late for your next lesson with Nya," said Sensei Wu.

"*Aw!* But when will I learn Spinjitzu?" Lloyd whined.

"Patience," Sensei Wu told him. "Your Spinjitzu will only be unlocked when the key is ready to be found."

Sighing, Lloyd went off to see Kai's sister, Nya, a samurai warrior.

Lloyd found Nya stroking the nose of a four-headed dragon. The great beast was sick.

"One day, he'll be yours," Nya said. "Ultra Dragon is meant for the Green Ninja to ride."

The dragon's four heads roared.

"Looks like he's feeling better," Lloyd said as the dragon flew off.

Lloyd was destined to become the legendary Green Ninja. Sensei Wu sent the ninja to find a better place to train him.

"These will transport you any place you want to go," Sensei said with a smile. "They are bus tokens!"

THE MEGA WEAPON'S POWER

Meanwhile, Lord Garmadon and his crew of Serpentine warriors flew high above Ninjago City aboard the *Destiny's Bounty*, the ancient pirate ship Garmadon had stolen from the ninja. He also had their magical Weapons. Combined, they formed the Mega Weapon.

Lord Garmadon only had one problem. He didn't know how the Weapon worked!

"We spotted something!" one of the crew members cried. He pointed to Ultra Dragon as it flew past the ship.

"Don't let him get away, you slithering idiots!" Garmadon yelled. He pointed the Weapon at the dragon. "Destroy!"

But the Weapon didn't do anything.

Garmadon stormed belowdecks. He pounded the Weapon on a table.

A secret door opened, and an old journal popped out. Lord Garmadon read the story of Captain Soto. The pirate and his crew had sailed the ship two hundred years before.

"This crew sounds like they knew how to handle a ship," Garmadon said. "I wish they were here to show these scaly idiots how it's done!"

Suddenly, the Mega Weapon began to sizzle and smoke.

"What is happening?" Lord Garmadon wailed. "It won't let me let go!"

Then he heard a voice overhead. "All hands on deck! I am Captain Soto!"

PIRATES ON BOARD

Lord Garmadon rushed to the deck. Captain Soto and his pirate crew had come to life! They waved their swords at the snakes.

"I asked for a better crew, and I got it," Lord Garmadon realized. "The Mega Weapon has the power to create!" But using it had left him very weak.

Captain Soto marched up to Lord Garmadon. "I be Captain Soto, Stealer of the Seas!" the pirate snarled. "We are taking back our ship."

Then he turned to his crew. "Lock him and all his reptilian friends in the brig!"

Lord Garmadon was too weak to fight back.
The pirates locked him and the Serpentine
warriors in the ship's jail.

On deck, Captain Soto discovered that his
ship could fly.

"This is too good!" He chuckled as they flew
toward Ninjago City. "Just wait till they get a load
of us!"

FOLLOW THAT SHIP!

Back in the city, the ninja had found a new place to train: Grand Sensei Dareth's Mojo Dojo. But Dareth was no Sensei Wu.

"I am a karate machine," Dareth bragged. But when he tried to show off his skills, he just got tangled up.

The ninja got busy training Lloyd. Cole showed Lloyd how to break a stack of boards.

Bam! Lloyd broke the boards — and the floor, too!

"With this power, you must be careful," Sensei Wu warned. "You must control it before it controls you."

Then the ninja heard screams outside. The pirates were attacking the city!

"You must stay here," Zane told Lloyd. "Your powers are not ready yet."

A bus pulled up, and the ninja hopped on.

"Follow that ship!" Kai told the driver.

DARETH WALKS THE PLANK

Grand Sensei Dareth wanted to impress the ninja. He jumped onto the pirate ship from a rooftop.

"Surrender, or face the brown ninja!" he cried.

"Pajama Man! Get him!" yelled Captain Soto.

Dareth's silly karate moves were no match for the pirates. They grabbed him and tied him up.

"Keep an eye out for any other masked Pajama People," Captain Soto told his crew.

Back in Ninjago City, Cole, Jay, Kai, and Zane knew that they needed disguises. They put on pirate costumes and sneaked onboard the floating ship.

Captain Soto was making Dareth walk the plank!

The ninja couldn't save Dareth. Captain Soto pushed him off the plank!

"Aaaaah!" Dareth screamed as he fell.

"Yee-hah!" Lloyd appeared, riding the Ultra Dragon! He swooped down from the sky. The dragon caught Dareth in one of its mouths.

WHO WILL WIN?

"Ninjago!" the four ninja yelled. They used Spinjitzu to transform into their ninja outfits.

Captain Soto looked confused. "More Pajama Men?"

"Ninja versus pirates," Kai said. "Who will win?"

Cole jumped across the deck. He used his scythe to slice the feather off Captain Soto's hat.

The battle had begun!

Three pirates surrounded Kai. He thrust his sword into the deck.

Whap! Whap! Whap! He grabbed the hilt and swung around, kicking the pirates away.

Another pirate charged at Zane. He held a sharp dagger in each hand.

Crack! Zane used his whip to send the pirate flying backward.

Kai and Cole fought off two pirates. Jay had an idea: He used his nunchuks to break open a gumball machine.

The gumballs spilled out onto the deck. *Splat!* The pirates tripped and fell down — and so did Kai and Cole.

"Oops!" Jay said.

A BARREL OF TROUBLE

"Ninjago!" Lloyd yelled. He jumped off the Ultra Dragon and landed on the pirate ship.

Captain Soto charged at Lloyd. Kai jumped between them.

"Lloyd! You're not supposed to be here!" Kai yelled. He stuffed Lloyd in a wooden barrel to keep him safe.

With the barrel over his head, Lloyd couldn't see where he was going. He accidentally bumped into the lever that dropped the ship's anchor.

Then he bumped into Kai. Kai jumped on top of the barrel, and they rolled across the deck together.

Kai fell off the barrel . . . and fell off the ship!

"*Whoa!*" he screamed.

He grabbed on to the anchor dangling from the ship. He clung to it as the anchor tore up the streets of Ninjago City.

A SURPRISE RESCUE

Back on the *Destiny's Bounty*, Captain Soto attacked Lloyd's barrel.

"Ninjago!" Lloyd cried.

He began to spin, turning into a green tornado of energy. The barrel exploded into pieces.

"I just did Spinjitzu for the first time!" Lloyd cheered.

Down below, Kai and the anchor were about to slam into a gas truck. If they hit it, the explosion would rock Ninjago City.

Up on the ship . . . *bam!* Captain Soto hit Lloyd from behind.

Lloyd fell into the lever that worked the anchor. It pulled the anchor back up to the ship — just in time!

Lloyd powered up with Spinjitzu — but he couldn't control his new abilities. Sizzling green light knocked down the mast of the ship. It crashed onto the ninja, trapping them all.

"You lose, Pajama People," Captain Soto said with an evil grin. "Now you're walking the plank."

Boom! Boom! Boom! The ship began to shake. The pirates looked up, and saw a giant robot stomping toward them.

It was Nya, piloting her giant samurai robot! She picked up the big mast and knocked down the pirate crew. Then she jumped out, slid down the ship's sails, and landed on Captain Soto.

"Who wins between pirates and ninja?" Jay asked. "It's samurai!"

The Ninjago City police rounded up the pirates. "That your ship?" an officer asked the ninja.

Lord Garmadon was flying away on the *Destiny's Bounty*. "You snooze, you lose!"

"Great," Jay sighed. "Lord Garmadon's back, and now he's got our ship?"

Cole mussed Lloyd's hair. "Well, at least we've got this little guy!"

Lloyd grinned. He couldn't wait until he could be the Green Ninja all the time!

LEGO NINJAGO
Masters of Spinjitzu

THE GREEN NINJA

KID STUFF

"We've been training all day," Lloyd complained to his four ninja friends, Cole, Jay, Kai, and Zane.

"We have to get you ready to face your father," Cole reminded him. Lloyd was the Green Ninja — the only one who could take down the evil Lord Garmadon.

"But the latest edition of *Starfarer* just came in to Doomsday Comics," Lloyd said.

"Sorry, Lloyd," Kai said, "but as the Green Ninja, you don't have time for kid stuff."

Nya ran onto the deck of *Destiny's Bounty*, the ninja's flying ship. "Guys! Lord Garmadon has broken into the Ninjago Museum of Natural History."

"Let me guess," Lloyd said. "This mission is too dangerous for me, right?"

"Right!" the four ninja agreed.

Inside the museum, Lord Garmadon held the Mega Weapon. It was a magical Weapon with the power to create.

"Behold . . . the Grundle!" Lord Garmadon cried. He pointed to a skeleton of a huge, fierce-looking beast. "It is now extinct. But when it roamed Ninjago, it could track any ninja."

RISE OF THE GRUNDLE

Lord Garmadon pointed the Mega Weapon at the Grundle skeleton.

"Rise, Grundle!" he commanded.

The Weapon sizzled with blue sparks. Purple energy waves flowed over the skeleton.

The four ninja burst into the museum. Garmadon's Serpentine warriors tried to stop them.

But the ninja were fast. They jumped on top of the Grundle. The snake warriors charged them. They knocked Cole, Jay, and Zane off the Grundle's back.

Kai threw his sword at Lord Garmadon, knocking the Mega Weapon from his hand. The purple energy faded.

"Not again!" Lord Garmadon wailed.

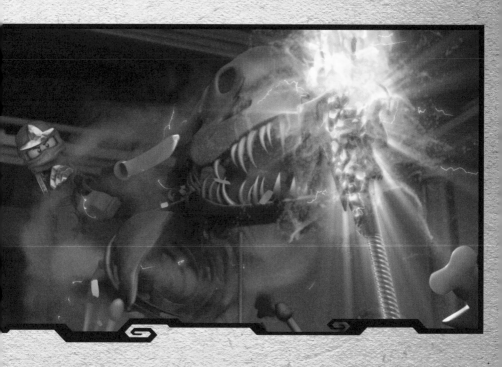

"*Ha-ha!* We stopped him! It didn't work!" Jay cheered.

Lord Garmadon ran off. His snake warriors followed him, carrying a golden sarcophagus along with them.

"They're stealing it!" Kai cried. "After them!"

The ninja raced out of the museum and onto the street. The sarcophagus was heavy, so the snakes dropped it and escaped.

THE INCREDIBLE SHRINKING NINJA

"I don't remember that sarcophagus being so big," Kai remarked.

"Did it grow?" Jay asked.

"Or did we shrink?" wondered Zane.

Suddenly, Kai noticed their reflection in a store window. "Uh, guys?"

"We *shruuuunk*!" Jay screamed.

It was worse than that. The ninja had been turned back into kids!

"I hate being a kid!" Cole wailed. "You can't drive. Nobody listens to you. Oh, no . . . bedtimes!"

"Garmadon must have made us younger with the Mega Weapon," Zane guessed.

At that moment, a police car screeched to a stop next to them.

"Looks like we caught the museum thieves!" the police officer said.

The ninja tried to explain what had really happened, but the police didn't believe them. Cole, Jay, Kai, and Zane spent the night in the police station.

Back at the ship, Nya and Sensei Wu were worried about them.

"Lloyd, you're in charge of the *Bounty* while Nya and I have a look around town," Sensei Wu told him.

ONE ANCIENT MONSTER

The next morning, the police brought the ninja and the sarcophagus back to the museum.

"Thank you," said the director. "But what about the Grundle?" He pointed to an empty display case.

"You don't think it just walked out of here?" Jay wondered.

"It is possible that Garmadon made the Grundle younger, too," Zane said, "and brought it back to life!"

Jay ran up to the grownups. "You guys have to believe us! The Grundle has been brought back to life, and it's on the loose!"

The director and the police just laughed.

"You boys wait here until we call your parents to pick you up," an officer told them.

"We gotta get out of here — like, now!" Cole warned the other ninja.

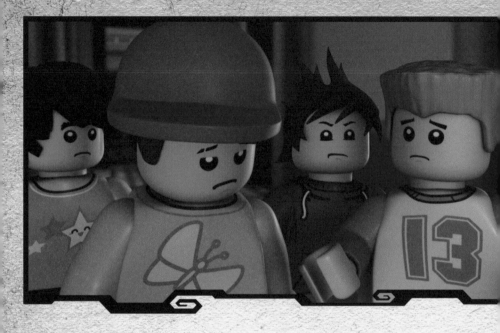

The ninja pretended to be part of a school group. They sneaked out of the museum.

"This is so humiliating!" Jay wailed.

"We can't use Spinjitzu in these bodies," Zane pointed out. "We are no match for the Grundle."

"Then we have to get back to the *Bounty*!" Kai told his friends.

THE GRUNDLE RETURNS

Rawr! As the ninja hurried away, a loud roar came from the museum. A huge, red beast with sharp claws and teeth jumped off the roof.

It was the Grundle! The great beast hated the sunlight. It stomped off to find a place to sleep until the sun went down. The people of Ninjago screamed and ran when they saw it.

The ninja didn't see the Grundle. They found a pay phone and called the *Destiny's Bounty*.

Lloyd answered the phone. "Where are you?" he asked. "Sensei is out looking for you."

"We can't explain now," Jay said. "Just meet us at Buddy's Pizza in ten minutes — and bring our weapons."

Ten minutes later, Lloyd strolled into the pizza parlor.

"*Pssst!* Lloyd!" Kai whispered.

"Beat it, brat! I'm on a mission," Lloyd said. He thought Kai was just some kid.

"It's me, Kai!" Kai told him.

Lloyd gasped. "Whoa! What happened? You're . . . small!"

Cole, Jay, Kai, and Zane explained how Lord Garmadon had brought the Grundle to life — and turned them into kids at the same time.

"We can't defeat the Grundle until we're back to full strength," Kai said. "We need to find someone who knows how to fight that thing."

Lloyd grinned. "I think I know just the guy!"

COMIC-BOOK HEROES

Lloyd brought the ninja to a comics shop.

"We're not gonna pick up your stupid comic, loyd," Kai complained. "This is serious business!"

Suddenly, Jay let out a happy cry. "Look! A ew issue of Daffy Dale!"

"Boys, this is Rufus McAllister, also known as Mother Doomsday," Lloyd said. "He owns this lace."

"Rufus, what do you know about the Grundle?" Lloyd asked.

"I know all about that extinct beast," Rufus said. "One, its thick hide can't be hurt by any weapons. Two, it only hunts at night. And three, the only way to defeat it is with light."

The ninja nervously looked out the window. The sun was going down fast.

"The Illuma Sword is the best weapon for fighting a Grundle," Rufus said. "That is, if you can get close enough to use it."

"We'll take the light swords," Kai said eagerly.

"Not so fast," said Rufus. "You'll have to win these swords in a *Starfarer* trivia battle."

"Sign me up!" Lloyd said.

Before the contest started, Lloyd got a message to Sensei Wu.

"There is only one person who can turn the ninja back to normal," Sensei Wu told Nya. They hurried to Mystake's tea shop and explained their problem.

"You need Tomorrow's Tea," the old woman told them. "I should have one here somewhere."

Back at the comic shop, the contest began. Lloyd and two other kids answered questions about the *Starfarer* comic book and its hero, Fritz Donegan. It came down to Lloyd and just one other player.

"Lloyd! Lloyd! Lloyd!" the ninja cheered.

"Here's your final question," Rufus said. "In the latest issue, how does Fritz Donegan escape the Imperial Sludge?"

"B-b-but I didn't read the latest issue," Lloyd stammered.

Just then, the lights in the comic shop flickered. The whole room began to shake.

"It's here," Kai whispered.

ATTACK OF THE GRUNDLE

"What's here?" Rufus asked nervously.

They all looked up at the glass roof. A huge, scary figure loomed above them.

Crunch! A huge, scaly foot stomped down, smashing the glass.

Everyone screamed and ran.

Crash! The Grundle fell through the ceiling. The ninja quickly ran and pulled on ninja outfits on display in the store. They each grabbed an Illuma Sword and charged the Grundle.

Hii-yaah! One by one, they attacked the Grundle, but the monster swatted them away like flies.

The Grundle hovered over them, its huge jaw open. Green slime dripped from its mouth.

"Aaaaah!" the ninja screamed.

"I'll take care of this," Lloyd said. He created a ball of energy in his hands and hurled it at the Grundle.

Swat! The Grundle knocked down Lloyd with its tail.

Suddenly, Nya and Sensei Wu burst through the door.

Sensei Wu held up a jar of glowing liquid. "Use this! It will turn time forward. You will grow up and the Grundle will turn back into a pile of bones."

He tossed the jar to Jay.

"Wait!" Cole cried. "What will happen to Lloyd? He'll grow old, too."

"Just do it!" Lloyd cried.

"We can't take away your childhood," Jay said. "It's not fair."

The Grundle charged at the ninja, and they fell backward. The jar flew out of Jay's hands and landed in Lloyd's lap.

Lloyd stood up. He threw the jar at the Grundle. It hit him in the nose, and a purple mist floated out.

THE GREEN NINJA

Purple light swirled, and the Grundle whirled around as the magic tea took effect. Then the great beast quickly crumbled into a pile of bones.

When the dust cleared, Kai, Jay, Cole, and Zane stood up. They were taller — and older.

"We're not kids anymore," Cole realized.

Lloyd slowly got to his feet. He was taller. His hair was thicker. His voice was deeper.

"I'm . . . older," he said slowly.

"The time for the Green Ninja to face his destiny has grown nearer," said Sensei Wu.

Lloyd looked at his friends. "I'm ready," he said confidently.

Lloyd's mind was racing. Now that he was older, he would be able to control his Spinjitzu better. But did he really have what it took to become the legendary Green Ninja?

Sensei Wu seemed to read his mind. "The time until the final battle has become shorter," he said. "But the Green Ninja has grown stronger!"

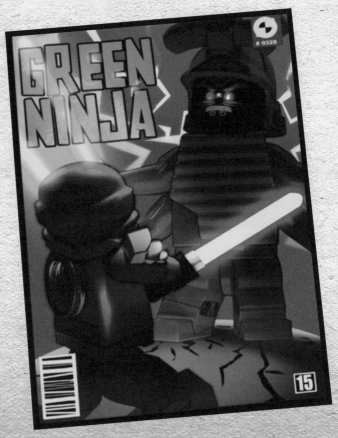

NINJAGO
Masters of Spinjitzu

ATTACK OF THE NINDROIDS

SCHOOL'S OUT

"Recess!" Cole cheered. "My favorite."

The teachers at Wu's Youth Academy hurried to the break room.

"All right, who took my pudding?" Jay growled. "It had my name on it."

Cole slurped up the last bite. "I didn't see 'motormouth' on it."

"I'm telling the headmaster," Jay whined.

Sensei Wu looked up from his tea. "Leave me out of it. I'm on break, too."

"Is anyone else mad Lloyd gets to fly around accepting awards while we're stuck here being teachers?" Jay asked.

Cole, Jay, Zane, and Kai had once been great ninja warriors. But there were no more enemies to fight. Lloyd, the Golden Ninja, had defeated the Overlord. The age of the ninja had come to an end.

"Did you guys hear the news?" asked Kai's sister, Nya, hurrying into the room.

"There's trouble?" Kai guessed.

"Danger?" Jay said.

"An emergency?" Zane hoped.

"No," Nya said. "We're going on a field trip to Borg Industries!"

FIELD TRIP!

The students and teachers piled into the school bus. When they arrived in New Ninjago City, everyone stared out the windows. Hover cars flew by. The city was filled with neon lights.

Cyrus Borg had invented many devices that had transformed old Ninjago City into a city of the future.

A droid welcomed them to Borg Industries. "I'm Pixal," she said. "Cyrus Borg's Primary Interactive Xternal Assistant Life-form." Pixal turned to Zane. "What does 'Zane' stand for?"

Zane stood tall. "Freedom — and courage in the face of all who threaten Ninjago."

"She means your name." Jay laughed.

"I guess I'm just 'Zane,'" said Zane. Like Pixal, he was a robot.

"Permission to scan?" Pixal asked Zane. Zane didn't know what that meant. But he felt important. "Uh . . . permission granted?"

Pixal's eyes scanned Zane's body. Then she said, "Mr. Borg would like to see the ninja on the hundredth floor."

MEET CYRUS BORG

The elevator doors opened into Cyrus Borg's office. "I would have guessed ninja would sneak in a window, not use the elevator," the inventor said.

"Isn't this the same place where the Overlord was destroyed?" asked Kai.

"Yes," said Borg. "What better way to send a message that we won't cower to anyone?"

"I wanted to give you a gift," Borg said.

"A gift?" Cole looked excited. "We won't say no to that. It wouldn't happen to be a cake, would it?"

Cyrus Borg pulled a sheet off a golden statue.

"Wow," Kai said slowly. "A statue . . . of yourself."

A MYSTERIOUS MISSION

The inventor pulled Kai to one side. "*Please, protect them with your life!* All of Ninjago depends on it!"

Kai didn't understand. "Protect? Protect what?"

"I should never have built here," Borg whispered. "You must go. . . . *He is listening*!"

"I'm sorry to cut this short," Borg told the others. "I hope you can show yourselves out."

"Guys, something weird is up with Borg," Kai said as they carried the statue into the elevator. "He was acting scared. He said we had to protect 'them' with our lives."

"Them?" Cole asked. "Who?"

"I dunno, but —" Just then, the statue tipped onto the floor and cracked open.

"There's something inside!" Zane said.

Cole picked up ninja outfits hidden inside the statue. "Why would Cyrus Borg give us new ninja outfits?"

Kai held up four strange weapons. "And what exactly are these?"

Suddenly, the elevator stopped. *"TECHNO WEAPONS LOCATED!!!!!"* a computer voice announced. *"Please drop the Techno-Blades."*

"Guys!" Kai yelled. "These must be the Techno-Blades. We have to protect them with our lives."

"Have it your way. Good-bye," the computer said.

A moment later, the computer released the elevator brakes. The elevator plummeted toward the ground!

Kai flipped up and slammed his feet into the top of the elevator. He had opened the escape hatch! "Going up?"

Cole, Jay, and Zane knew what they had to do. *"NINJAAAA-GO!"*

The four ninja used Spinjitzu to leap to safety.

ROBOT ATTACK!

Meanwhile, Pixal was showing Nya, Sensei Wu, and their students around Borg Industries. Suddenly, Pixal's eyes began to glow red. "This will be the end of your tour."

Flash! Lasers fired at the group. Sensei Wu and Nya fought back.

Something evil was controlling the machines inside Borg Industries!

Luckily, the ninja were ready for action.

"Gotta say it," Jay said. "I love the new threads."

Suddenly, evil security robots surrounded them, firing lasers.

"Oh, yeah?" Kai said. He aimed his new Techno-Blade at the robots. "Two can play at this game. *Hi-yah!*"

But nothing happened. The Techno-Blade didn't work!

Kai shook it. "What's with these things? How do we turn them on?"

The security guards fired again. A blast shattered the window. The ninja fell through and plunged toward the ground!

"Hold on!" Cole yelled to the others. He was holding a fire hose! The ninja swung through the air together.

"Ready to crash the party, boys?" Cole asked. They smacked into a window. *Splat!*

The four ninja slid down the side of the building onto a window-cleaning platform.

RETURN OF
THE OVERLORD?

The ninja knew they had to figure out who was trying to get the Techno Weapons. Kai thought it was the evil Overlord.

"But how?" Cole said. "We all saw Lloyd defeat him."

Zane nodded. "Defeat, yes. But can he be destroyed?"

A Hover-Copter zoomed toward them.

"I don't know," Jay said. "But *we* can!"

"Cole, throw me!" Zane yelled.

Cole threw Zane onto the Hover-Copter. Zane landed on top and slammed his Techno-Blade into the cockpit.

The Blade lit up. White lightning glowed all around the Hover-Copter. Now it was a Ninja-Copter!

"The Blade hacked the Hover-Copter's system," Jay cried. "Zane controls it!"

Zane zoomed over to pick up Cole, Kai, and Jay. The ninja had students to rescue!

The Ninja-Copter hovered outside Borg Industries. Inside, their students were still under attack. The Ninja-Copter's lasers fired through the windows.

The students cheered. They were safe!

Soon the students were back on the school bus.

Kai turned to Nya. "Get to the Academy as fast as you can, sis. Find Lloyd. We need the Golden Ninja."

"What about you guys?" Nya asked.

"We must stay to protect the people," said Sensei Wu.

HACK ATTACK!

The four ninja and Sensei Wu huddled together. "These Techno-Blades can hack into their systems," Kai said.

Jay grinned. "Whaddaya say we do a li'l Hack Attack?"

"Zane, Kai — you take to the skies. I want Cole and Jay on the ground. I'll do what I can for the people," said Sensei Wu.

"*Ninjaaa-go!*" the four ninja cheered.

Zane steered his Ninja-Copter into the sky.
Kai rode on top. "Oh, I want *that*!"

Kai jumped onto a jet fighter and slammed
his Techno-Blade into it. Fire ripped across it, and
it turned into a Kai-Fighter!

Suddenly, a hologram of Cyrus Borg appeared.
Borg told Kai that the ninja needed to get the
Techno-Blades out of the city or the Overlord
would destroy them.

New Ninjago City was in grave danger. The ninja were under attack! Dozens of armed robots were on their trail.

Jay flipped toward an evil security tank. He jammed his Techno-Blade into it. Blue lightning shot over it. Now the tank was Jay's!

Nearby, Cole swung onto a Security Mech. He slammed into it with his Techno-Blade. It turned jet black. Cole was in control!

"We have to get the Techno-Blades out of the city," Kai told the other ninja.

"But what about Sensei?" Zane asked. Sensei Wu had been helping the people of New Ninjago City escape.

"I'll pick him up," Kai said.

But Sensei Wu was surrounded by hostile robots!

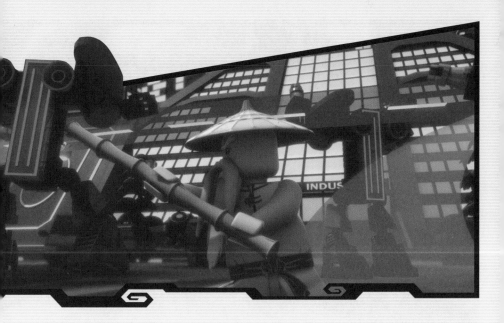

Suddenly, a golden blast blew everyone back. It was Lloyd, the Golden Ninja!

Evil laughter filled the air. "Golden Ninja. We meet again."

"Overlord," Lloyd said. "I defeated you once; I'll defeat you again."

"Oh, I don't want to fight," the Overlord said. "I just want your power!"

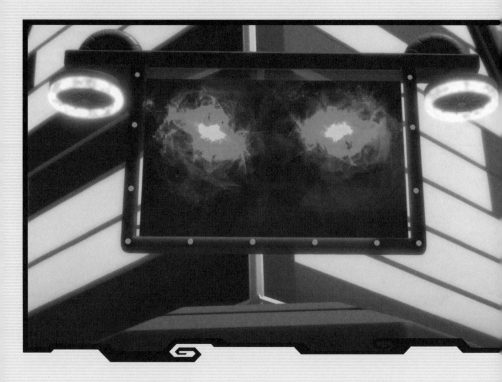

A DARING PLAN

"Lloyd, your power is making him stronger," Sensei Wu cried.

"We need to get you and the Techno-Blades out of the city," Kai added.

"I have an idea," Sensei Wu said quietly. "Listen closely. . . ."

A moment later, the ninja all spun to their vehicles. *"Ninjaaaa-go!"*

Sensei Wu dashed across the rooftops of New Ninjago City. He was carrying a bundle covered in cloth.

"The sensei has the Techno-Blades!" the Overlord's voice boomed.

In no time, Sensei Wu was surrounded by Hover-Copters. He opened his bundle. It was empty! Sensei's plan had worked.

The other ninja zoomed out of New Ninjago City in their new vehicles. They had escaped with the Techno-Blades!

"We have to go back for Sensei," Lloyd said.

Kai nodded. "We will. When you are safe."

"The Overlord wants these weapons," Cole told Lloyd. "But he also wants you."

"We will come back to New Ninjago City," Zane added. "And when we do, we'll be ready."

Back in New Ninjago City, evil had taken over. "The city is ours," the Overlord said. "It's time we create our own ninja."

Pixal loaded a scan of Zane into the computers. "Upgrade complete." Borg's factory began to produce hundreds of ninja droids — *nindroids*!

Cole, Jay, Kai, Zane, and Lloyd were about to face some serious competition.

NINJAGO
Masters of Spinjitzu

TECHNO STRIKE!

NINJA ON THE RUN

In New Ninjago City, evil forces were at work. "Tell me where the Golden Ninja is!" the Overlord screamed at Sensei Wu.

Nindroids had been searching for all five ninja for days. But they hadn't found them—or the Techno-Blades.

"I'll never tell you," Sensei Wu vowed.

"You might not . . . but your memories will!" the Overlord cackled.

"This is a perfect place to lay low," Lloyd told Cole, Jay, Kai, Zane, and Nya. He looked around the monastery. "No robots, no cameras—no problems."

"Lloyd?" a voice said. It was Misako, Lloyd's mom. "What are you doing here?"

Lloyd gave her a hug. "The Overlord's back, and New Ninjago City has fallen under his control. He has Sensei Wu."

"Where is Lord Garmadon?" Kai asked.

"Here, he is Sensei Garmadon," Misako said. "Come in . . . but no weapons. Garmadon has sworn an oath never to fight again."

"But we're supposed to protect the Techno-Blades with our lives," Kai said.

"You guys go ahead," Zane offered. "I'll watch over them."

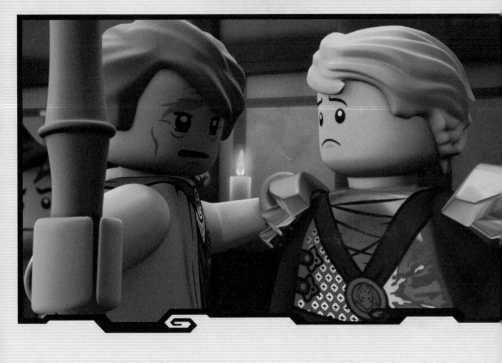

FIGHT WITHOUT FIGHTING

Inside, the ninja found Sensei Garmadon.
"Son, so glad you could join us," he said.
"Tonight's lesson is the Art of the Silent
Fist—to fight without fighting."

Garmadon asked Lloyd to demonstrate.

As the other ninja practiced, Zane jumped up. The Techno-Blades were missing!

There was a rustling sound in the trees. He was not alone!

Zane raced through the orchard. Finally, he came face-to-face with . . . "Pixal! What are you doing here?"

"Discontinuing an old droid," the Overlord's assistant said, attacking him.

Kai heard Pixal and Zane fighting. "The Techno-Blades!"

The other four ninja followed him outside. "How did she find us?" Cole asked.

"She was only doing what she was programmed to do," Zane said. He touched his Techno-Blade to her forehead, and Pixal's eyes turned green.

"How did you find us?" Zane asked.

"They've mined Sensei Wu's memory," Pixal said. "The Overlord wants the Golden Ninja and his power!"

"What makes the Techno-Blades so important?" Kai asked.

"They can reboot the system and destroy the Overlord for good," Pixal explained.

Suddenly, Pixal remembered something.
"I didn't come alone!"
　　"Who else is with you?" Jay asked.
　　"Nindroids," Pixal said.
　　"NINDROIDS?!" the ninja cried.
　　They were surrounded!

SNEAK ATTACK!

The Nindroids pounced. Though there were more of them, the ninja were smarter fighters.

Sensei Garmadon joined the battle. He fought without fighting—and it worked. The Nindroids began to crash into one another!

Lloyd powered up his golden energy, but Nya stopped him. "No! Your power only strengthens them!"

"Let's get out of here!" Nya shouted.

"Anyone want to clear a path?" Jay asked.

"I've got an idea," Cole said. He led them to a waterwheel, and the ninja hopped on. The waterwheel rolled down the hill, scattering all the Nindroids in its path. It was the perfect escape!

"If the Overlord wants my son, I'm not letting him out of my sight," Garmadon said.

Lloyd nodded. "But if he wants me, and the Techno-Blades are the only thing that can stop him, shouldn't we split up?"

Nya nodded. "You two go find shelter in my Samurai X cave. The rest of us will shut down the power in New Ninjago City."

Back in New Ninjago City, the Overlord was furious. "What do you mean they're not there?!" the Overlord screamed.

"We've been tricked," General Cryptor said.

"Your Nindroids have failed, General Cryptor . . . but my next creation won't!" the Overlord growled.

STEALTH MISSION

The ninja found a sneaky way to get past the Nindroids guarding New Ninjago City. They hid inside a circus caravan!

"We owe you one," Kai said, hopping out of a magician's box. "Thanks."

The magician waved his magic wand. "We can get you to the Storm Farms, but you're on your own with the Power Substation."

"So, Nya," Cole said, "can we really destroy the Overlord and his Nindroids by simply flipping a switch?"

"Cripple them, yes . . . destroy, no," Nya answered. "Once we've powered down his army, we still need to reboot the central computer with the Techno-Blades."

While the others planned their attack, Pixal helped put Zane back together. He'd been hurt badly during the Nindroid battle.

"Thank you for repairing me," Zane said, smiling. "I guess an old Nindroid like me is no match against the newer models."

THE SAMURAI X CAVE

Out in the desert, Lloyd and Sensei Garmadon followed Zane's falcon. "The Samurai X symbol!" Lloyd gasped.

Lloyd pressed the symbol, and the creature's giant skull yawned open. There was a secret passage!

Inside were dozens of weapons and vehicles. Garmadon spotted a Samurai Raider—a perfect getaway vehicle!

Lloyd tried to hop into the driver's seat, but his dad blocked him. "I swore off fighting . . . not driving."

"Where to now?" Lloyd yelled as they zoomed away.

"As far away as possible!" Garmadon said.

POWER DOWN

Meanwhile, the ninja had reached the Overlord's power station. Nindroid guards surrounded it.

"This is where all of Ninjago gets its power," Zane told Pixal.

"If we want to get in, we have to stay out of sight. We can't take them all on," Nya said.

"I'll stay back," Pixal offered. She would keep watch.

As the ninja sneaked toward the power station, General Cryptor warned his Nindroids, "Keep your eyes out for ninja."

Then Cryptor stopped and laughed at one of his droids—it was tiny. "Look at you! Ran out of metal, did they? I will call you Min-droid. Ha-ha!"

Meanwhile, the ninja had found their way to the station's control room. In the center, something was glowing behind glass.

"That's the power core," Nya said. "Shut that down and it's lights out for the Overlord. If only we knew which switch . . ."

They pushed buttons, but nothing happened.

"There has to be an easier way!" Cole said.

While the ninja were hunting around inside the control room, the Nindroids were lining up outside the door. They were ready to attack!

"Knock-knock . . ." General Cryptor said quietly.

Suddenly, an alarm rang out. Pixal had seen the Nindroids!

"Nindroids!" Nya shouted. "Our cover is blown!"

"Pixal!" Zane ran out of the control room. As he opened the door, the tiny Min-droid rolled in.

"Great, now they come in fun-size!" Jay groaned.

Garmadon and Lloyd were also under attack. The Overlord had created a powerful new machine—a giant MechDragon! It was racing toward Garmadon and Lloyd.

"He's gaining on us!" Lloyd yelled.

Back at the power station, General Cryptor had taken Pixal prisoner.

Zane fought his way through an army of Nindroids. *"Ninjaaaa-GO!"* He took his Techno-Blade and spun through the air.

"You're the original Nindroid," General Cryptor laughed. "Nothing more than a tin can with feelings."

Nya and the ninja were still trying to shut down the control center. But Min-droid kept attacking them.

"Hack him with the Techno-Blade!" Kai shouted to Cole.

Cole swung his weapon—and missed. "I'm trying! I gotta hand it to this little runt. He doesn't know when to quit."

LIGHTS OUT

The Min-droid fired a laser at them. Cole ducked. The blast hit the power core, cracking the glass around it.

"That's it!" Kai said. "Fight without fighting!" He waved at the Min-droid. "Hey, half-pint! Over here!"

The Min-droid fired another laser. Kai ducked—and the glass cracked more.

"We need more Nindroids!" Cole shouted.

Nya opened the door to the control room. The Nindroids swarmed in and began to shoot at the ninja.

The ninja dodged the laser fire. With each shot, the glass around the power core splintered more and more.

"It's working!" Nya cried.

Elsewhere in Ninjago, Lloyd and Sensei Garmadon were still trying to escape the Overlord's MechDragon. The dragon was getting closer and closer. . . .

Back at the power station, Min-droid lunged at the ninja. They ducked out of his way, and—
He smashed into the power core! POW!

In an instant, the robotic dragon crashed to the ground. All the Overlord's other creations shut down. New Ninjago City went dark.

"We did it!" Kai shouted. They had defeated the Nindroids—and the Overlord!

Out in Ninjago, Lloyd and his father knew their friends had succeeded—for now, at least.

"Is it safe to go back?" Lloyd asked.

Garmadon shook his head. "They may have turned off the power, but they still need to reboot the system. Until we know the Overlord is gone for good, we must keep moving."